"There's my Zoe," Grandma says, waving me into the kitchen with a floured hand.

"Can I help?"

"Wouldn't be the same without you," she says.

I wash my hands and stand beside her at the table. Grandma shows me how to knead dough into a ball that will rise like magic.

Her hands tell a story if you listen.

"I was just a little girl like you when Momma taught
me how to make cinnamon bread," she says.
"Ingredients are only part of it. You've got to get the rhythm."

Push and pull. Push and pull.

I try to do like Grandma but the dough bunches instead of glides. It's sticky instead of smooth. I frown at my hands and wonder if they will ever move like hers.

"Like this," she says, sprinkling flour like fairy dust
and placing her hands over mine. We use the
heels of our palms to push the dough forward.
Then, we fold to pull it back again.

Push and pull.

Push and pull.

Until it's just right.

I place the dough into a greased bowl
Grandma covers with a cloth.

"Making bread takes time," she says.

So we sit and wait.

We sit and talk.

Her hands tell a story if you listen.

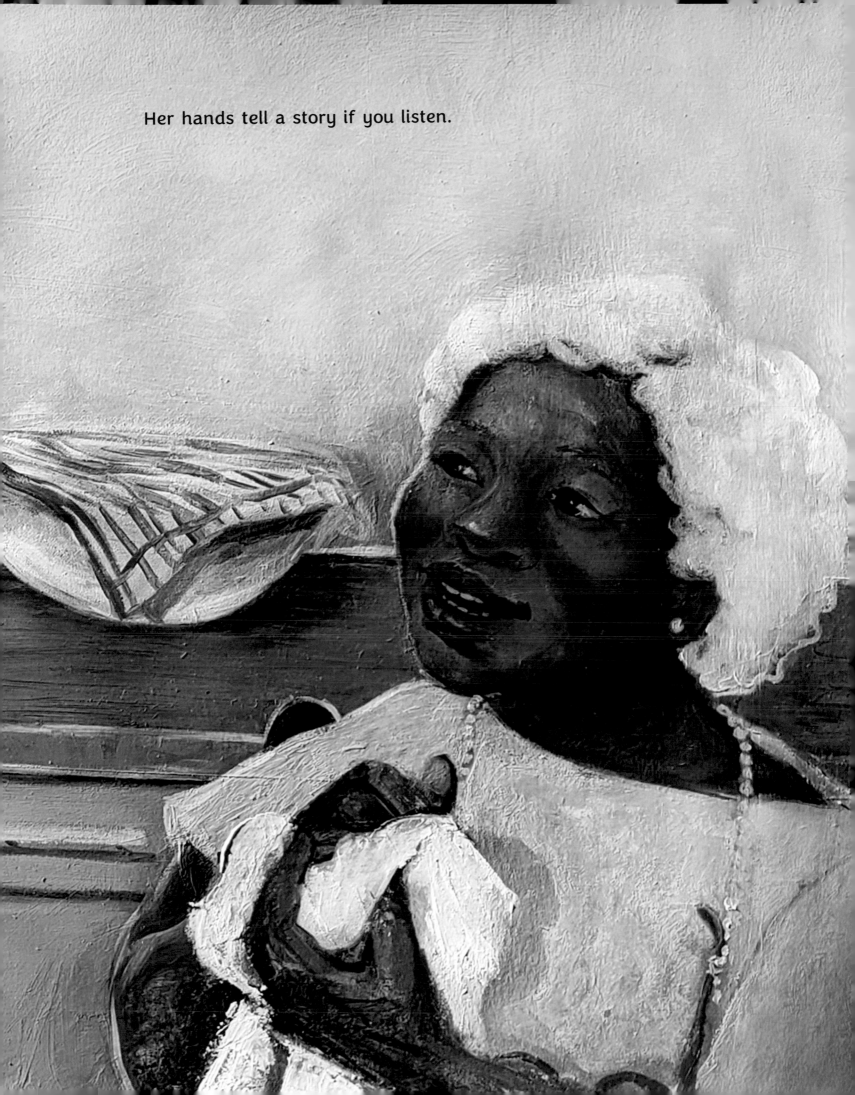

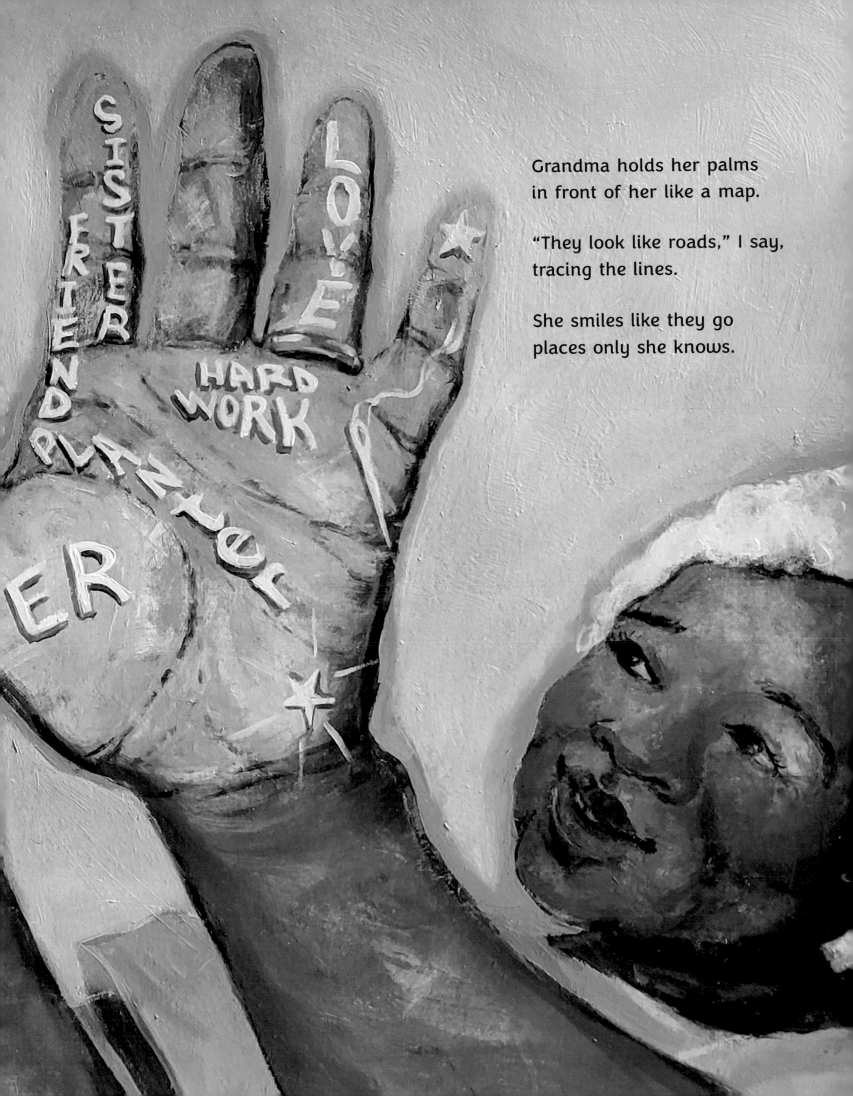

Grandma holds her palms
in front of her like a map.

"They look like roads," I say,
tracing the lines.

She smiles like they go
places only she knows.

"Wasn't easy," she says. "Typing and filing until my
hands ached. Then heading to the studio at night.
Some people said I should just be happy I was working.
But I had a dream of dancing on stage."

I picture Grandma in the spotlight. Head raised toward
heaven, her hands weave a world without saying a word.
Then, she takes off, leaping and twirling through time and
space. Her fingers are branches, stretching toward the sky.

I look at my hands and wonder what stories they will tell.

Where will they go? What will they learn?

Eating at their house always makes me feel special. Gifts from their garden steam in china dishes—squash and onions, collard greens, candied yams. Tangy smells tickle my nose and make my mouth water.

I wonder if one day my hands will grow something too.

Before I know it, we need to check the dough. I can't believe how big it has swelled. We flatten it, then dust it with cinnamon sugar. Next, we roll it up and lay it in the pan. I cover it with cloth so it can rise again.

"Let's get some air," Grandma says.

Outside on the glider, the wind whistles as
Grandma rubs my hand soft as a whisper.
I hear murmurs of her hands flowing and
dancing, praying and planting, stroking
my hair when she thinks I'm asleep.

Then something happens.

I look at my hands, really look at them, for the first time.

I can see memories in every line.

Clapping games with friends.

Drawing my dreams.

Building and baking.

"Time for the oven," Grandma says, rising to go inside.

While we wait for our bread to be ready, I think about the power in my hands. They can turn pages, color, and create. What will tomorrow bring?

When Grandma puts down her crossword puzzle,
I jump up and race to the oven. It's time.

She cuts hunks of our cinnamon-swirled bread. The spicy
aroma makes me wiggle. I spread butter that melts into each
nook. We take a bite and slap our hands together. Grandma
stares at my fingers like she's seeing something new.

"You have my hands," she says.

Our fingers are long and skinny. Sweet brown
like sugar. Made for holding and reaching.

"But you'll go places I've never been,"
Grandma says with pride.

I see my hands raised in victory as I cross
the finish line. I see them making music.
I see them writing about Grandma and me.

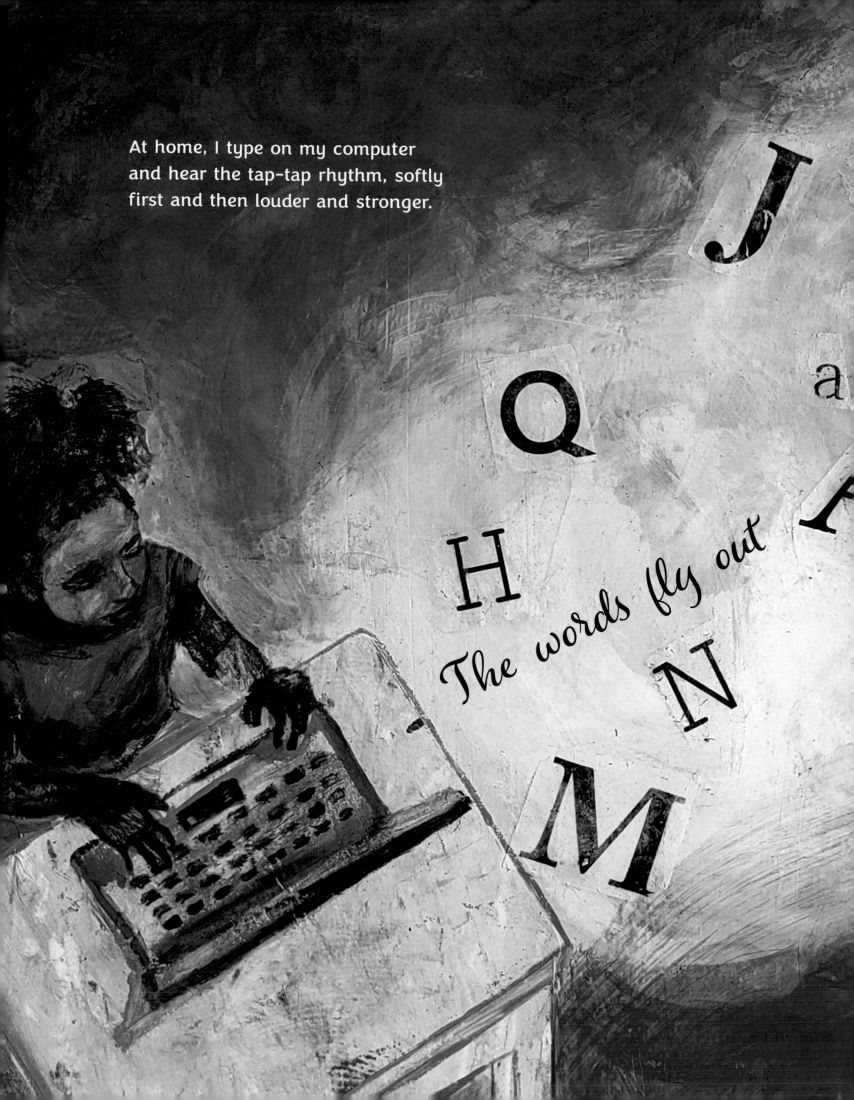

At home, I type on my computer
and hear the tap-tap rhythm, softly
first and then louder and stronger.

The words fly out

J

Q

H

M

N

like they're sailing on a breeze.

Zoe and Grandma's Cinnamon Bread

INGREDIENTS:

Bread dough:

Packet of active dry yeast (should be 1/4 ounce)

1/2 cup warm water (105-115 degrees)

1 teaspoon sugar

1 egg, lightly beaten

1/2 cup of warm milk

3 tablespoons of softened sweet cream butter

1/2 teaspoon salt

1/4 cup sugar

3 cups all-purpose flour

Cinnamon filling:

2 tablespoons melted butter

1/2 cup brown sugar (optional)

liberal amount of cinnamon sugar (as much as you desire)

DIRECTIONS:

1. Grease a 8 1/2 in. X 4 9/16 in. loaf pan.

2. Dissolve yeast in warm water (105-115 degrees). Mix in 1 tsp. sugar. Let sit for 5-10 minutes or until it becomes foamy. (If yeast doesn't foam, the water may be too hot, or there may be a problem with the yeast. Start over with a new packet.)

3. Combine yeast mixture with egg, warm milk, sweet cream butter, salt, and sugar. Mix in flour a 1/2 cup at a time. Should form a soft dough.

4. Flour the surface where you're working. Lightly flour your hands too. Knead for 5 minutes until dough is elastic and smooth.

5. Place ball of dough in a greased bowl. Turn over once so that the top of the dough is greased. Cover with a damp cloth. Put in a warm place to rise for one hour or until it doubles in size.

6. Punch down the dough. Roll it out on a floured surface into a rectangle (8 inches by however long you'd like).
   Note: The longer you roll it out, the more swirls it can make.

7. Brush melted butter across the rolled-out dough. Liberally spread the cinnamon sugar (or cinnamon sugar and brown sugar) across the surface.

8. Roll tightly, jelly-roll fashion. Pinch the ends to seal.

9. Place in greased loaf pan, seam-side down. Cover with damp cloth. Let rise for one hour.

10. Place in oven at 350º for 30 minutes.

Let cool and enjoy!